Squishy McFluff's
Camping Adventure

Pip Jones · Ella Okstad

faber

Hellllooooo! Can you SEE him, the best EVER pet?
Have you imagined him hard enough yet?
That's it! HERE he is! You can give him a pat . . .
Meet Squishy McFluff, my INVISIBLE cat!

'We've got an exciting weekend up ahead,
but camping's a "SERIOUS business",' Dad said.

'We must be prepared! From the time we arrive, we'll need our base instincts and skills to survive.'

Yes, roughing it out in the wild might be tough, but nothing's too scary for Squishy McFluff!

Our campsite is cool! Frilly flowers! Tall trees!
Twittering birdies! And bumbling bees!

We've got a great spot by a babbling brook
and it's full of invisible fish, Squishy. LOOK!

Yay, Dad's unpacking!
Oh, he's taken GREAT care
to bring the essentials –
like his comfy armchair,

the radio too, and
his apron and wok,

the rug from the hall and
our mantlepiece clock,

his slippers and

"TWANG!
    TWANG!"

his trusty guitar . . .

'THE TENT! Ava!
    Why is it not in the car?'

'We did see the tent, Dad, at home on the porch
(it was next to the sleeping bags, gas stove and torch).

We were going to tell you to pack it, but then
we thought camping's BEST
when you build your own den!

Wait for me, Squishy, while I roll up my sleeves.
Together we'll gather some branches and leaves!
Oh Daddy, our instincts
will make you
so proud . . . !'

'What's that racket?
My EARS! It's ever so loud!'

'Hello! I'm Idris. My dog's called Farida.
We're fab at dens and will help! But I'M leader.'

'I'm Ava! And thanks, but we're fine on our own.
We're experts AS WELL! Um, I don't mean to moan,
but please tell your dog to stop yapping like that!
It's hurting my ears and she's scaring my cat!'

'What cat? I can't see it. There's just nothing there.'

'HUMPH! Squishy McFluff is incredibly rare!
You have to be special to spot him, you see.
Which is why, as a stray, Squishy chose me!'

'He can't be much fun! An invisible pet?
Farida does tricks you can SEE, and I bet . . .'

'We're a TEAM, me and Squishy, so may I suggest
we each make our OWN den and see whose is best?

Right, Squish. Let's do this. We'll find what we need:
branches and ferns and Dad's hammock, agreed?

Then ropes to secure things, umbrellas, our boat,

then brambles to keep people OUT!

And a MOAT!'

'Ava!! Try using a rope which is longer,
then tie some more knots to make your den stronger.
Oh, SEE? Watch Farida! She's fetching my stuff!'

'I doubt she's as helpful as Squishy McFluff.'

'Ava!! Just widen that entrance some more,
then borrow my surfboard to use as a door!

Farida Pup Puppington! SEE? She's so clever!
Watch her! She's surely the greatest pet ev . . . ?'

'Well . . . !

Squish has just whispered his latest grand plan.
You'd probably both like to help if you can.

We're going on a search for invisible wood.
It'd make YOUR den stronger! It's ever so good!'

'Shh! What was that!? I hear branches breaking!
Thundering footsteps, and now the ground's quaking!

PAWS!
GREAT,
BIG
TEETH!

Look, SEE it?
Right there?

A GUZZLING,
GROZZLING

GRIZZLY
BEAR!!!'

'It'll flatten the tents! And eat everyone's food!
Those guzzling grizzly bears are SO RUDE!'
'Our DENS! Oh, we really must stop it, but how?'

'Fear not, Idris! Squishy knows what to do now!

OI, BEARY!

OI, BEARY!

You might be a bear
with sharp claws and gnashers,
but Squish doesn't care!

He'll nip at your tail,
stuff your nostrils with petals
and tickle your snout
with these prickly nettles,

then bounce on your belly,
then CHASE YOU AWAY!
Shoo, naughty bear!

Well, that showed it . . .'

'HOORAY!

You're right, Ava! Squishy is so quick and clever.

He scared the bear off, he's the bravest cat ever!

He must be a brilliant pet, I can tell!'

'But how do you know . . . ?'

'I CAN SEE HIM AS WELL!'

'We're **both** good at dens. I'm wondering whether
we should all be a team and join them . . .

For my mum. E. O.

For Cami, and for brave and brilliant girls everywhere. P. J. Xx

Faber has published children's books since 1929. T. S. Eliot's *Old Possum's Book of Practical Cats* and Ted Hughes' *The Iron Man* were amongst the first. Our catalogue at the time said that 'it is by reading such books that children learn the difference between the shoddy and the genuine'. We still believe in the power of reading to transform children's lives. All our books are chosen with the express intention of growing a love of reading, a thirst for knowledge and to cultivate empathy. We pride ourselves on responsible editing. Last but not least, we believe in kind and inclusive books in which all children feel represented and important.

First published in the UK in 2023
First published in the US in 2023
by Faber and Faber Limited
Bloomsbury House
74–77 Great Russell Street
London WC1B 3DA
faber.co.uk

Printed in India

Text copyright © Pip Jones, 2023
Illustration copyright © Ella Okstad, 2023

The moral rights of Pip Jones and Ella Okstad have been asserted.
A CIP record for this book is available from the British Library.

ISBN 978–0–571–35038–4

10 9 8 7 6 5 4 3 2 1

FSC
www.fsc.org
MIX
Paper from
responsible sources
FSC® C016779